PIRATES!

To two big girls, Madelaine and Louisa,
two big boys, Michael and Ronnie,
a great big dog, Ivan,
and my mom.
—DW

For Mark and Gretchen and Colleen and Ridley,
in the name of friends in love and love in friends.
—K. H.

First Edition 1 2 3 4 5 6 7 8 9 10

Library of Congress Cataloging in Publication Data   Woychuk, Denis. Pirates! / by Denis Woychuk ; pictures by Kim Howard.   p.   cm.   Summary: When Mimi is stolen by pirates, Gustav uses his wit and skill to rescue her.   ISBN 0-688-10336-7. — ISBN 0-688-10337-5 (lib. bdg.)   [1. Hippopotamus— Fiction.   2. Mice—Fiction.   3. Pirates—Fiction.]   I. Howard, Kim, ill.   II. Title.   PZ7.W8885Pi   1992   [E]—dc20   91-33876   CIP   AC

Mimi & Gustav in
PIRATES!

by Denis Woychuk
pictures by Kim Howard

Lothrop, Lee & Shepard Books
New York

During the day Gustav worked as a waiter at a downtown cafe. Mimi taught ballet to children. In the evenings they liked to take walks by the sea.

One night, when the moon was just a small
banana in the sky, they walked along the pier,
holding hands.

"When I close my eyes," said Mimi dreamily,
"I can imagine myself the captain of a big ship."

"Me too," said Gustav, and he closed his eyes.
Suddenly Mimi's hand slipped from his.

"Help!" she cried as she was lifted through the air in a giant net. She felt quite dizzy.

Moments later the net dropped onto the deck of a ship. A flashlight snapped on.

"Aha, my proud beauty!" cried a gruff pirate. "The circus will pay plenty for a dancing hippo, or my name isn't Captain Crook."

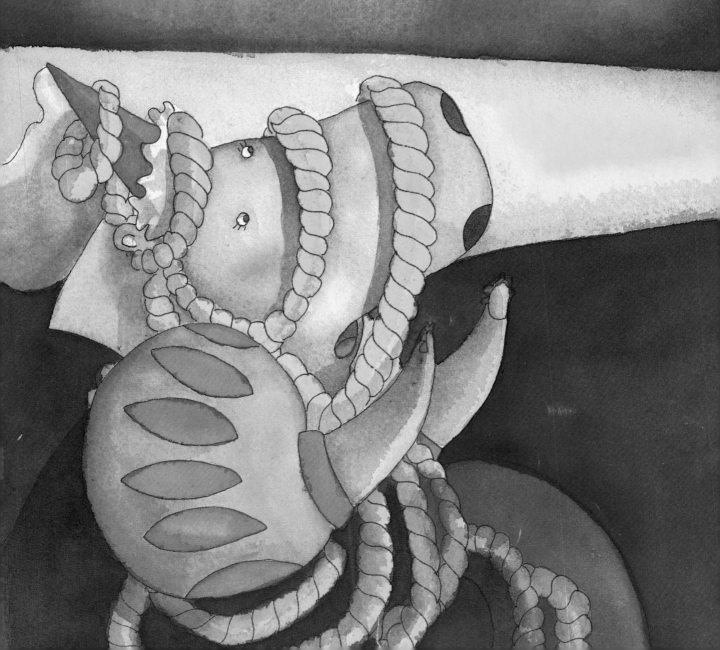

The captain and his sidekick locked Mimi in a cage. Then they weighed anchor and set their sails.

Mimi could feel the ship rocking on the waves. Where were they bound? she wondered. What would become of her? And where was Gustav?

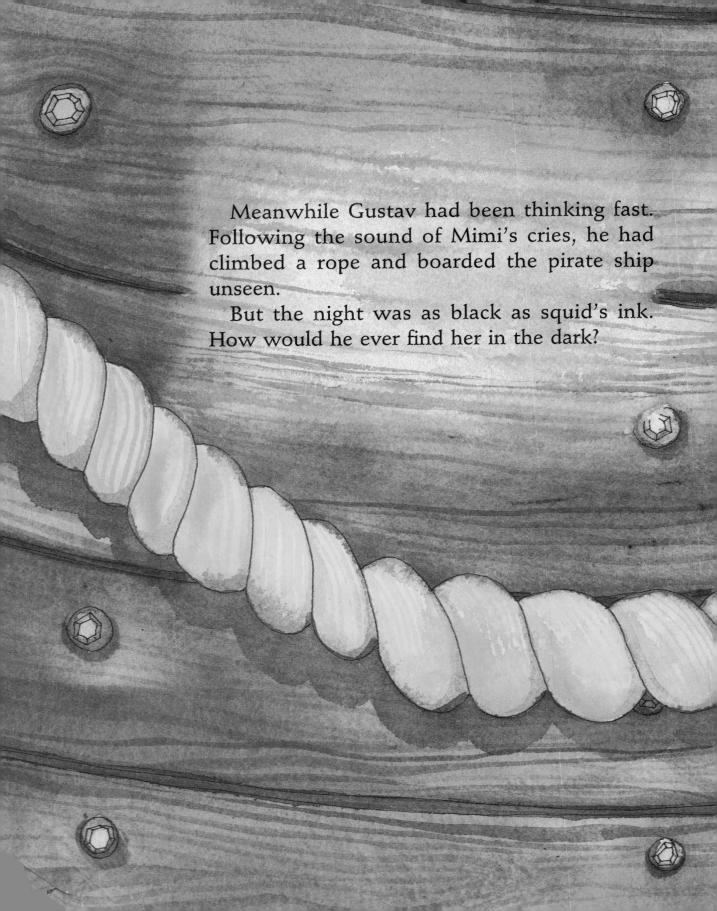

Meanwhile Gustav had been thinking fast. Following the sound of Mimi's cries, he had climbed a rope and boarded the pirate ship unseen.

But the night was as black as squid's ink. How would he ever find her in the dark?

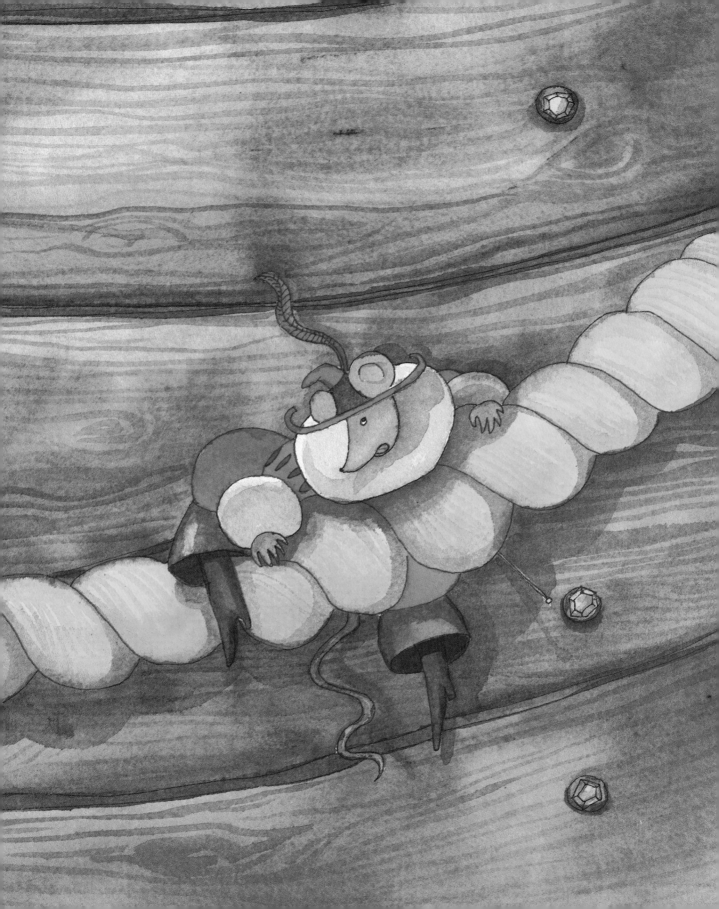

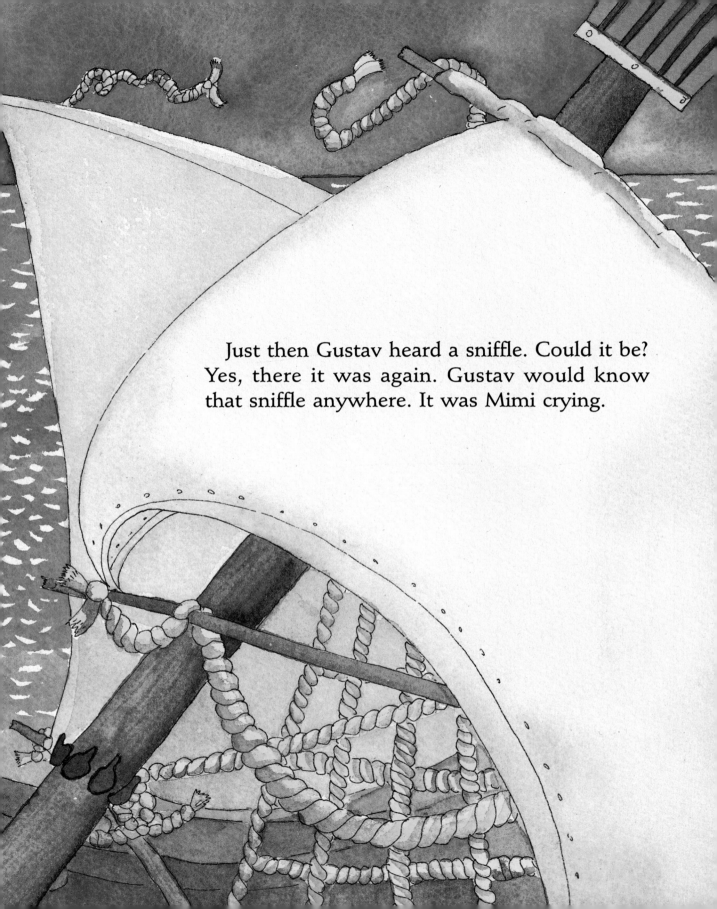

Just then Gustav heard a sniffle. Could it be?
Yes, there it was again. Gustav would know
that sniffle anywhere. It was Mimi crying.

Gustav stealthily crept straight to the cage. But alas, though Gustav could squeeze between the bars, Mimi could not.

Fortunately the pirates' parrot was friendly. "There's a key to the cage in the captain's cabin," it squawked. "Watch out for the cat."

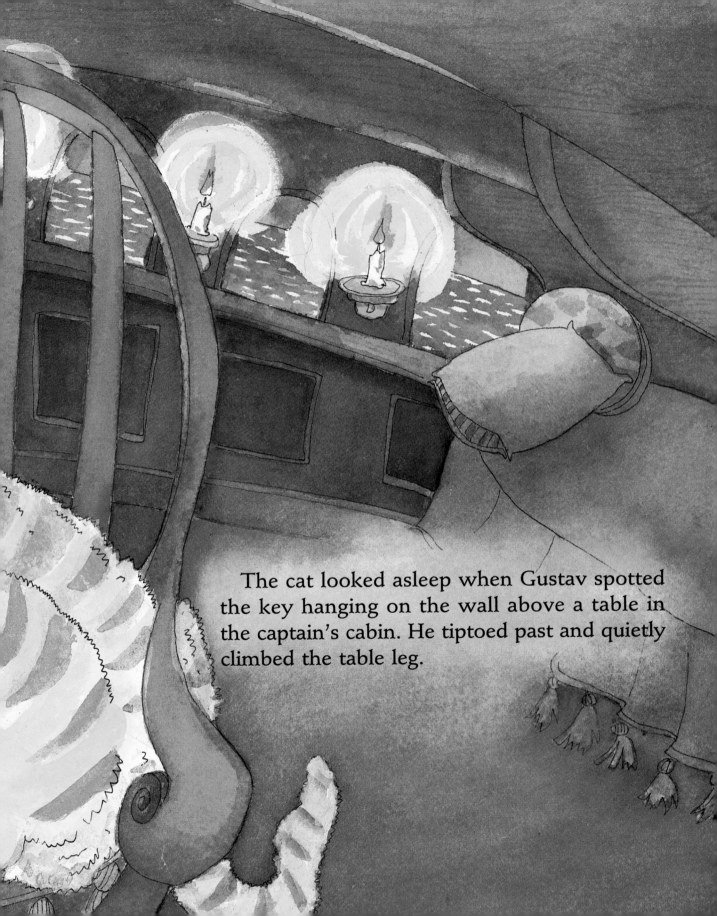

The cat looked asleep when Gustav spotted
the key hanging on the wall above a table in
the captain's cabin. He tiptoed past and quietly
climbed the table leg.

But it had been only a catnap. Catching the scent of mouse, the cat was on the table in a single leap. Gustav, however, had not spent his youth as a musketeer for nothing. Grabbing the key from the wall, he wielded it like a sword. The cat swiped. Gustav danced lightly to the side and stabbed her paw with the key. The cat swiped again.

Gustav dodged and stepped in. *Bop!* A direct hit, right on the nose. The cat was not hurt, but she was stunned. Never had she seen such a mouse!

Gustav took advantage of the moment. He leaped from the table and dashed across the floor and out the door, remembering to shut it behind him.

Gustav scaled a cage bar and fit the key into the lock. He gave a mighty turn and the cage door swung open. Mimi was free! But this was no time to celebrate.

Hand in hand, they dashed onto the deck and dove neatly into the water. But Captain Crook had spotted them. *Boom!* A cannonball splashed into a nearby wave.

"Swim for it!" Mimi shouted.

"But Mimi!" cried Gustav. "I can't swim!"

"I will save you! Grab my tail and climb onto my back!"

Mimi was a strong swimmer. It wasn't long before Gustav spotted land and they waded ashore.

"It's good to be back on dry land," said Gustav.

"Oh, Gustav," said Mimi. "It's good to be anywhere with you."